First published in 1940
by Faber and Faber Limited
3 Queen Square London WC1N 3AU
This edition first published in 1989

Printed in Great Britain by
W.S. Cowell Ltd Ipswich

Text © The Alison Uttley
Literary Property Trust, 1940, 1989
Illustrations © Graham Percy, 1989

British Library Cataloguing in Publication Data is available

ISBN 0–571–15294–5

Quality Printing and Binding by:
Faber and Faber Ltd.
3 Queen Square
London, WC1N 3AU, England

Sam Pig and the Dragon

Of course Sam Pig had always believed that Dragons were extinct, like Unicorns and Ogres. Otherwise he would never have entered Dragon Wood. It was a pretty little wood, filled with primroses and bluebells in the spring, and many birds nested in the trees. Nobody knew why it was called Dragon Wood, and even old Badger laughed at the name. Butterfly Wood or Dragon-fly Wood seemed more suitable for such a charming spot, for many brilliant butterflies flitted among the open spaces, and green dragonflies hovered and darted over the little pond. Sam often went there with his net, but either the meshes were too large or the gossamer threads of the net were too fragile, and the little flying creatures always broke away.

One day he went to the wood with a basket for primroses. They grew in clusters under the shade of the rocks, and he soon filled the little rush basket. Then he sat down on a convenient rock. It was rough and black, but ferns grew in the crevices, and lichens patched the surface in orange-coloured discs like coins spilled over it. The sun had warmed it, and Sam lay back staring at the blue sky, watching the clouds through the young leaves of the overhanging trees. He shut his eyes and let the sun beat down in its spring warmth upon him. He was filled with content, and he was nearly asleep when he was startled by a slight movement under his body. The rock seemed to rise and fall in slow even motion.

He sprang up alarmed, and looked round. There was nothing unusual. The rock lay there, dark and massive, the ferns glowed like transparent green water, the clouds floated in the sky above. Only one thing was different. A little disturbed earth had fallen upon the mossy ground near the rock, and the primroses had spilled from the basket.

Sam Pig rose slowly to his feet. 'I think it was an earthquake,' he said to himself.

He listened, holding his breath, and there came a deep sigh. Perhaps it was a sigh, perhaps it was the wind moaning. Then he thought he saw an eye flash at him. Perhaps it was an eye, perhaps it was the sun in the glittering rain pool. Sam didn't wait any longer. He picked up the basket, stuffed the primroses in it, and went home. He turned his head now and then, and saw nothing alarming, but he couldn't help wondering.

'I've been to Dragon Wood,' he announced when he entered the house. 'And I heard – and I felt – and I saw –'

'Well?' cried Tom impatiently. 'What did you hear and feel and see? A dragonfly?'

'Nothing,' said Sam, hesitating. Then he added, 'But it was like something. A nothing that was like something.'

He didn't go near Dragon Wood again for months. He stayed away till the flowers had gone and the trees were beginning to change the colour of their leaves.

'I want some blackberries for jam,' said Ann one autumn day. 'Go to Dragon Wood and pick some, Sam. There's plenty on those bushes, and nobody ever goes there.'

'Dragon Wood,' said Sam slowly. 'Dragon Wood. Well – yes, I'll go, Ann. I'll take my fiddle for company. I feel a bit queersome in Dragon Wood when I'm all alone.'

'All right. Take your fiddle, Sam. Maybe you will wheedle the blackberries off the bushes by playing to them, and I'm sure the rabbits will enjoy your music,' laughed Ann.

So away went Sam. There were the finest blackberries on a bank where the trees were scarce, and the rocks broke through the earth. He picked the juicy fruit and filled the little basket, and ate a good few himself. Then he put the basket under a tree and wandered on with the fiddle under his chin, playing a tune as he walked. The wood seemed to listen, the birds cocked their heads and sang in reply, the trees waved their branches in slow lazy rhythm, and Sam Pig felt happy and carefree. He saw the rock which had once moved and there it was, solid as the earth, weather-worn and black with rain. Yet when he stared at it he thought it was somehow different. He could trace a kind of shape about it, a bulging forehead, heavy brows, and even eyelids, long slits cut deep in the rock, half covered with bright moss. He didn't feel inclined to sit upon it, but he went on playing, to make himself brave.

Now whether it was the sweetness of Sam's music, or the warmth of the autumn sun, I do not know, but the bracken began to wave, the earth quivered and shook, and the rock was slowly uplifted. It was a scaly dark head, very large and long, with half-shut eyes concealing a glimmer of light like stars in a cloud. Ferns and lichens rolled away, the little silver birch trees toppled over, and a large oak tree crashed to the ground as the huge beast stretched itself. Then it opened its mouth and yawned, and it was as if a pit had opened in the wood. Sam gave a shrill cry and backed away. The Dragon blinked its liquid eyes and looked at Sam. The glance was kindly, and Sam stopped.

'Hallo,' said the Dragon, in a voice which seemed to come from under the earth, so deep and rumbling it was. 'Hallo, I've been asleep, I think! What time is it?'

'About twelve o'clock,' said Sam in a shaking voice, and he glanced up at the sun. 'Yes. About twelve.'

'What day?' asked the Dragon, after a long pause.

'It's Saturday,' faltered Sam.

'I mean, what year,' said the Dragon, very, very slowly. 'It's always Saturday. What year is it?'

'Oh, it's – er – er – nineteen hundred and something,' stammered Sam. 'I can't remember what.'

'Too soon,' growled the Dragon, like low thunder. 'Too soon. I've waked too early. I had to sleep till twenty hundred.'

'When did you go to bed?' asked Sam, forgetting his fright in his curiousity.

'Oh, in the year a hundred or thereabouts. The Romans made it so uncomfortable for me, marching about with their legions and tidying everywhere, I went to sleep and covered myself up. But I've waked too soon. My sleeping time is two thousand years. Have they gone yet?'

'Who?' asked Sam.

'The Romans,' said the Dragon.

'I'm not sure,' said Sam. 'But there's only me and Badger and my brothers and Sister Ann living near. Not any Romans.'

The Dragon seemed to ponder this, and there was a long silence.

'Hadn't you better go back to bed again?' asked Sam, staring uneasily at the great head. 'I'll cover you up.'

'Now I'm awake I'll just look about me,' said the Dragon. 'I like your music, young fellow. Play to me again.'

The Dragon yawned once more and showed its

long white teeth and its curving scarlet tongue. A faint blue smoke came from its nostrils, and it blinked and snorted.

'I can't breathe properly,' it grumbled. 'Play to me. My throat's sore. I must have got a chill in the damp ground. I expect it's been raining and snowing a bit while I've been sleeping there. I hope I shan't get rheumatics.'

Sam played his fiddle and the Dragon waved its head in slow awkward jerks, up and down, stretching its scaly folds, loosening the thick stony skin.

'That's better,' said the Dragon. 'You've done me good. I am not so stiff now, and my throat's more comfortable.'

Sam thought it was time he went home, but the Dragon had taken a liking to him. So when he started off, the Dragon followed after. Sam quite forgot his blackberries, and he walked quickly, not caring to run from the great beast. The Dragon scarcely seemed to move, but it arrived as soon as Sam.

'You'd best wait outside,' said Sam. 'They'll be a bit surprised when they see you. I'd better warn them. You see, you are too big to come into our house. We're not used to Dragons, but I'm sure everybody will be pleased to see you.'

The Dragon agreed, and it lay down in the field.

'I am much obliged to you,' it murmured in its deep rumble. 'I can breathe easily now. The change of position has done me good, and the ancient warmth inside me has wakened.'

Indeed it had! From its nostrils came a cloud of smoke and from its mouth spurted little flickering flames of fire.

'You're burning,' cried Sam. 'Shall I fetch some water from the spring?'

The Dragon shook its great head, knocking over the palings and the clothes-props in the crab-apple orchard. 'I never drink water. It puts me out. It's my nature to smoke. You'll get used to it.'

So Sam ran up the garden path and flung open the door. He was breathless with excitement. 'Ann! Tom! Bill!' he shouted. 'There's a Dragon outside.'

'Dragon!' scoffed Bill. 'Where are the black-berries? We've been waiting to make the jam. Why have you been so long?'

'There's a Dragon outside,' repeated Sam. 'I forgot the blackberries because I found a Dragon. I've brought it home with me. At least,' he corrected himself, not wishing to appear boastful, 'at least, it followed me. It's waiting outside.'

They stared in amazement at their young brother, and then they ran to the door. They could see the monster lying outside the garden gate, with its head in the lane and its tail in the

paddock. Little spirals of smoke came from the Dragon's nostrils, and its green eyes stared unblinkingly from the rocky head.

'Now, Sam,' said Ann, crossly, 'whatever did you bring a Dragon home for? You went for blackberries, not Dragons. What shall we do with it? We haven't a stable for it, and we can't have it in the house.'

'Stable! House!' scoffed Tom. 'If it whisks its long tail our house will be knocked clean over, and if it moves its head the orchard will be destroyed. It is singeing the crab-apples already.'

'It may ripen the crabs,' said Sam eagerly. 'It's very warm.'

'If it breathes hard we shall be roasted into roast pork,' said Bill, mournfully.

'But it's a nice gentle Dragon,' interrupted Sam, 'and I found it. I think it is lonely.'

'Well, go and speak to it,' said Tom, shrugging his shoulders.

Sam went down the garden to talk to the Dragon. It lay very still, breathing quietly, staring at the blue sky.

'You had best stay outside,' said Sam, 'and please behave yourself, for Sister Ann is rather worried about you.'

The Dragon nodded so hard that Sam was blown backward by the force of the wind. It promised to behave if only Sam Pig would let it stay. It curled itself round the house and garden, and shut its eyes.

Then the rest of the Pig family went closer to look at it. Its head was near the garden gate, but not near enough to scorch it. Its tail swept under the wall, and away into the orchard. There was just room to walk past without getting harmed by the Dragon's breath. They agreed it was quite a nice beast, and very unusual.

Badger was much surprised when he came home that evening. He hummed and hawed as Sam told the exciting story. The Dragon was dozing, and Badger watched it.

'It belongs to an ancient family,' said Brock. 'It is probably the last one left in the land. It will be lonely without companions. It's a pity you waked it, Sam. It may cause us a deal of trouble. I'm not used to Dragons.'

'I am,' said Sam. 'It likes my music and it's quite tame. Let us keep it, Badger. I will be its companion.'

The little pig looked imploringly at Brock, and Brock hummed a little tune and gazed at the Dragon. It was rather awkward having that great hot beast so near to one's garden gate. Nobody would come to visit them, but of course it was as good as having a watchdog. In any case Brock didn't know how to get rid of the Dragon. There it was and there it would stay.

They soon got used to having a Dragon round the house. It was very tame and gentle, and no trouble at all. The little animals of the woodland played on its scaly back, rabbits leapt upon it, and robins perched on its eyelids. The Dragon lay very still, just breathing, opening an eye now and then when Sam played to it, smiling at the little pig.

Ann Pig stretched a clothes-line over its head, from the lilac tree in the garden to the wild sloe in the orchard. Then she hung out the washing to dry in the fire of the Dragon's breath. The clothes dried even in wet weather, which was a great saving of time and trouble. The crab-apples

ripened, the flowers sprang up anew in the hothouse of the Dragon's presence. When the days were short and winter came, the Dragon kept the house warm as toast. The snow fell and the frosts made the earth like iron, but the Dragon lay there, a warm comforting beast. They sat on its back in the coldest weather, and picnicked on the moss-covered scaly tail. The Dragon told them stories of long ago, tales of the days when wolves and wild boars and shaggy bears lived in the country. It told them of its brother Dragons, and its ancient mother, famous throughout the world for her strength. Then a tear of loneliness would trickle down its face, a tear so hot that steam rose from it. Sam rose to fetch his fiddle to cheer the sad beast, and the Dragon sighed and winked away the tears, and forgot its ancient greatness.

Brock brought his friends to see the wonderful visitor and everyone said the pigs were honoured by this King of Reptiles who was so considerate and kind.

Spring came, and Sam sat on the garden gate with his fiddle. The cuckoo called and the nightingale sang. The Dragon moved its head in its sleepy bliss and puffed the white flames from its mouth. It was always content, never asking for anything, neither eating nor drinking – a perfect guest.

Then one fine day a cow disappeared. Sam Pig had seen it coming up the lane, and he ran indoors to fetch his milking-pail and the three-legged stool. When he came out the cow wasn't there, so the pigs had no milk for their tea. It was very strange, and Sam hunted in the fields for the lost cow. She had completely vanished.

A few days later another cow went. She had been feeding in the meadow, near the Dragon's tail. The farmer's dog came to look for her and he eyed the Dragon suspiciously. The Dragon's eyes were shut, and the great beast lay with a look of happiness on its stony face.

The sheep-dog spoke to the Pig family. 'It's my opinion,' said he, sternly, 'it's my good opinion that that there Dragon knows something about our Nancy. Aye, and about our Primrose too, as went the other day. She was a good milker was Nancy. Well, you can't have it both ways. You can't keep a Dragon, and have your gallon of milk regular.'

'It can't be the Dragon,' protested Sam. 'Why, there's a blackbird's nest on its back, and there's a brood of young rabbits living beneath it. Everybody knows our Dragon, and it's as gentle as a dove.'

'That's as may be,' returned the dog. 'I'm only telling you. I've my suspicions. Cows can't fade away like snow in summer.'

The pigs talked it over and Sam decided to sit on the Dragon's back and keep watch. The Dragon never noticed who was on its back; it was too thick-skinned to feel any difference. Sam had once seen the roadman empty a cart-load of stone upon it when he was mending the lane, but the Dragon never flinched. Only the cart-horse shied, and was restive till he was led away.

So Sam sat light as a feather on the Dragon's back, and kept guard. He felt he was acting the traitor's part to his friend, and he carried his fiddle ready to play a tune to soothe the Dragon's feelings, if he had misjudged it.

Up the road came a cow, going to the milking. It loitered here and there, picking up a blade of grass, snuffling at the herbage. When it got to the Dragon it put out its red tongue and licked the salty scales of the beast. Sam waited breathlessly. The Dragon snapped open its mouth, and in a twinkling the cow had gone, like a flash down the flaming red lane of the Dragon's throat.

'That settles it,' said Sam quietly, and he slid to the ground, and went round to face the Dragon.

'You'd best be going back to bed, Dragon,' said he in a determined way, but the Dragon opened its sleepy eyes and gazed lovingly at Sam.

'Not yet, Sam dear,' said the Dragon. 'Not yet. I'm so happy where I am, dear Sam Pig.'

Sam was not to be cajoled. He took his fiddle and played a marching song.

'Follow me,' he commanded the Dragon. 'Fall in and follow me. Quick march! One! Two! One! Two!'

The Dragon stirred its great length, heaved its heavy body from the orchard and meadow grass, and shuffled after Sam.

Back to Dragon Wood Sam led the Dragon. He took it right to the place where he had found it. There was the hollow, where its head had lain, and the wide ditch where its body had rested.

'Now go to sleep,' said Sam. 'I'll play a lullaby, and you must shut your eyes and go fast asleep.'

Sam played a gentle rocking tune and the Dragon gazed at Sam. A great warm tear rolled down the Dragon's cheek, and then another tear fell with a splash on the ground. The Dragon shut its eyes obediently and settled itself in the moist earth. Soon there was no movement in the vast body. The Dragon was asleep.

Sam covered it up with leaves and grasses and planted ferns and spring flowers upon its back.